W9-AKA-395

MAY   1989

JEFFERSONVILLE TOWNSHIP PUBLIC LIBRARY
JEFFERSONVILLE, INDIANA

JE
Z
Z 655 ch

#
15793638

R901747

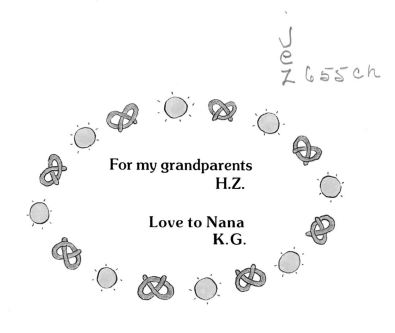

**For my grandparents
H.Z.**

**Love to Nana
K.G.**

Text copyright © 1988 by Harriet Ziefert
Illustrations copyright © 1988 by Karen Gundersheimer
All rights reserved. Printed in Singapore for Harriet Ziefert, Inc.
First published in the U.S.A. in 1988 by Harper & Row, Publishers, Inc.,
10 East 53rd Street, New York, NY 10022. Published simultaneously
in Canada by Fitzhenry & Whiteside Limited, Toronto

Library of Congress Cataloging-in-Publication Data
Ziefert, Harriet.
     Chocolate mud cake.

     Summary: Molly and her little sister Jenny bake
a make-believe cake out of mud, twigs, and berries when
they spend an afternoon at their grandparents' house.
     [1. Sisters—Fiction.   2. Play—Fiction]
I. Gundersheimer, Karen, ill.   II. Title.
PZ7.Z487Ch 1988   [E]   87-12139
ISBN 0-06-026883-2
ISBN 0-06-026892-1 (lib. bdg.)

CHOCOLATE MUD CAKE

BY HARRIET ZIEFERT
ILLUSTRATED BY
KAREN GUNDERSHEIMER

Harper & Row, Publishers

I'm Molly.
Jenny's my little sister.
We're playing at Grandma
and Grandpa's house today.

I'm busy cooking.

Jenny wants to know
what I'm making.
"A chocolate cake!" I say.

"This is going to be
a very yummy cake!"

I crumble up some dirt.
Jenny says, "Me too!"
So I let her be my helper.

I mash up the big lumps of dirt.

And I let Jenny find the little
stones and throw them away.

I tell Jenny just to dribble the water.
But she dumps it in and makes mush.

I show her how to fix the cake with sand.

I add nuts and berries
for crunch.
Jenny adds leaves.

I let Jenny mix and stir.
Then it will be my turn.

Mix and stir.

Stir and mix.

Cake in the pan.

Pan in the sun.

Now it's baking!

I check the cake.
"Jen-ny! Grand-ma! Grand-pa!
The cake is done!
Come and see!"

I show Grandma and Grandpa the cake.
"I hope you'll give me a big piece!"
  says Grandpa.
"Me too!" says Grandma.

Jenny looks at the cake.

She looks at me.

She says, "*You* eat the cake!
I want a pretzel!"

Grandpa gives Jenny a pretzel.
I get one too.

Two pretzels!
One for me.
One for Jenny.
Happy eating!